ALL IN

A HEROES COLLECTION
SHORT STORY

ALEXANDRIA BLAELOCK

BlueMere Books
MELBOURNE, AUSTRALIA

For permission requests, please contact
enquiries@bluemerebooks.com.

Ordering Information:
Discounts are available on quantity purchases. For details, contact orders@bluemerebooks.com.

All In/Alexandria Blaelock
paperback ISBN: 978-1-922744-27-2
digital ISBN: 978-1-922744-28-9

ALL IN

Rosa Velázquez forced herself up the last five steps, and believing the sound wouldn't travel through the solid door at the top, stood panting on the red brick landing.

Her thighs ached, and her feet screamed in agony.

God, she was out of shape.

Would she ever be that fit again? With her feet that scarred, it didn't seem likely.

The door was plain, stained a rich jarrah red, with an old-fashioned black steel lever handle.

And a tiny, handwritten tag in a black steel frame beside the door; Jude Webb, Bespoke Shoes.

He was supposed to be the best in Melbourne.

Which was why she'd climbed three flights of stairs to his Hardware Lane workshop.

Despite her misgivings about the anonymous donation of his services.

Quite frankly she was suspicious of both of him and her benefactor. Always assuming they were, in fact, different people.

But her feet hurt with every step she took, and the lure of handmade shoes, with extra cushioning in the sole was too tempting to stand on her principles and refuse.

She tapped on the door.

No sound of acknowledgement came from within.

She thumped it as hard as she could.

Still nothing.

Admittedly, her thumping barely made much more noise than her tapping.

She pulled the handle down, leaned into it with her shoulder, and overbalanced as it turned out to be ridiculously easy to move.

"I'll just be a moment," he said, his back turned to her, "please take off your shoes and take a seat on the chair."

The man inside was much younger than she'd expected for a Master craftsman.

With his thick dark hair, she'd say early thirties.

He was wearing a thick, white cotton shirt with the sleeves rolled up, and a blue tweed vest with matching trousers.

He looked like he belonged in a different century.

She looked at him doubtfully, seemingly engrossed in shaving the leather from the sole of one shoe with a sharp and slender bladed knife. One tanned finger testing the edge of the cuts.

A lock of his shoulder-length hair fell from where he'd tucked it behind his ear, brushing his collar. Was that the corner of some kind of tattoo peeking out from behind the collar?

She stepped up on the platform and took her shoes off, placing them neatly side by side next to the chair, and her bag next to them.

She clasped her scarred hands between her skinny jean-clad thighs and looked around the room.

The red wooden workbench was placed under the crittal windows.

Their black steel frames were a nice contrast against the red brick of the exposed walls, the red wood of the exposed beams, and the white ceiling liner that reflected the dim winter light around the room.

Jude sat at one end of the bench, on a matching adjustable stool with three legs, a small lamp shedding extra light on his work. A combination of hand and handheld power tools were neatly arranged in racks under the windows.

At the other end of the bench, there was a small laptop, connected to an electronic payment machine and a small printer.

A couple of speakers, also connected by wires, sat on the edges of the pillars that supported the ceiling joists. Quietly playing some kind of Latin dance music.

Jarrah racks with blank pine lasts seemingly arranged at random lined one wall, a second held racks of fragrant leather, and the last supported large machinery of some kind.

Rosa snuck a look at Jude's shoes.

Highly polished black leather, elasticated sides, almond-shaped toe, Cuban heel.

Nice pair of Chelsea boots.

She had almost the same pair back home, though off the rack, not made to measure.

Not leather, and not comfortable either.

Not that she could bear to wear them anymore. It was probably time to throw out all her shoes.

Jude swivelled on the seat to look at her, wiping his hands on a grey apron she hadn't noticed until then.

He took it off and hung it on a peg by the bench.

"Sorry about that," he said, walking towards her holding out his callused hand, "I'm Jude Webb."

She stood to take it, "Rosa Velázquez." His hand was warm and strong, almost completely enveloping her own.

"Can you roll up your jeans?"

She looked at her legs, "I'm afraid not."

A smile crossed his face so quickly she wasn't sure she'd seen it.

"I need to see and assess the condition of your ankles. Would you be comfortable taking them off and wearing a blanket instead?"

She looked uneasily down at her legs. He couldn't see it, but the scarring was severe.

"Or perhaps you'd like to come another day?"

She squared her shoulders; she hadn't walked up all those stairs just to walk straight back down them with nothing to show for the effort.

"No, it's okay. Give me the blanket."

He handed her the blanket, and she clutched it to her chest, "I'll wait outside, let me know when you're ready."

«« « • » »»

Jude shut the door and leaned his back against it. Almost as if he had a wild creature trapped inside the workshop and didn't want to let it out.

Which in a way, he did.

Rosa Velázquez was like a ray of light shining into his workshop. Outshining the dim winter light leaking through the windows of his art deco workshop.

Though in the day's defence, it was cloudy and midwinter; it could barely compete against the fluorescent lighting let alone Rosa Velázquez.

Her name had seemed familiar when the appointment came in, so he'd looked her up on the internet.

Two years ago, Rosa Velázquez, a secretary waiting for the bus on her way to work, had run *into* a burning building and saved the life of a mother, then *gone back in* to save her two children.

She'd been lucky, clearing the house with the last child in her arms, just moments before it collapsed.

Somewhat less lucky, she'd been wearing a polyester suit and synthetic leather shoes, which had melted into her skin in addition to the burns from the fire.

Rosa was literally a hero. A bona fide hero with several medals to prove it.

Rosa startled him by opening the door a crack.

Her hair was cropped close to her head, and her serious, impossibly blue eyes showed a mixture of fear and stubbornness.

"You can come in now."

He tucked his hair behind his ear again and grinned at her, the light blanket folded over her blouse and around her body like a sarong.

He leaned on the door, and as she backed up, gestured for her to precede him.

She sat on the chair again, and he knelt before her.

"I understand you're looking for oxfords?"

She cleared her throat, "I was until I say your boots."

"Okay," he grinned as he saw her looking again, "why don't you tell me exactly what you're looking for?"

He looked up at her as she started talking, marvelling at her delicate facial features as she talked about how much pain she felt walking, and how she wanted beautiful shoes because she was sick of wearing clumpy ugly shoes, and how her feet weren't as flexible as they had been, and she worried she'd never walk properly again.

There was not one word that stuck inside his head, but he was beginning to form an idea of the shoes he was planning to make her.

"Would you be wearing socks or stockings with these shoes?"

"Um, I have some compression socks."

He grunted.

First, he picked up her shoes and examined them inside and out to see where the wear was, and how she was carrying her weight.

"May I?" he said, gesturing at her feet.

She nodded, and he picked up her left foot, rubbing and bending it to see its formation, checking for calluses as well as heel and toe deformities.

Aside from the obvious scars.

Jude started moving up her leg, under the blanket, and she gasped and stiffened.

He stopped immediately, "I need to check your ankles too."

After a moment she relaxed, and he continued, testing the thickness of her ankle, and the thinness of her bones.

And maybe he went a tiny bit further up her calve than he needed to, but the scarring was misleading.

"Did anyone talk to you about scar massage?"

"No, not really."

He frowned, "then this might hurt a bit," he moved her ankle from side to side, and bent more firmly on her feet.

She held it as long as she could, and then squeaked in protest.

"I'm sorry," he said, then started again with her right foot.

"About the compression socks?" he said putting her foot back on the floor.

She leaned across to her bag, pulled them out and handed them to him.

He put his hand in the sock and stretched it out, "good, just a little light compression at this point."

"How is that good?"

"Ordinary socks just hold your foot in place, these ones have a little compression around the arches, which means the shoes don't have to do as much work."

"Ah."

He grinned, "it also means the shoe can be a little more relaxed, and maybe, I could do a low-heeled Mary Jane, or even a Chelsea Boot."

The hope in her eyes was heartbreaking.

"Why did you ask about scar massage?"

"Do your scars still itch?"

"A bit?"

"Massaging the scars can help reduce the itching, and relax the scars, making them more flexible. Would you like me to show you?"

She nodded.

"Okay, let me finish up measuring first."

He pulled the socks onto her feet with practised ease, and drew around her feet, noting the measurement of the widest part of her feet, the middle of the arch, where the foot and leg meet, and the length of her heel.

"I'll be right back," he said, shoving his papers aside, and ducked out of the room.

《《 • 》》

Rosa was surprised by how gentle his hands were.

And how he looked at her like she was the centre of the universe.

She liked it.

And she liked the way his hazel eyes deepened to a chocolate colour when he looked up at her for longer than a glance.

She was so used to the sight of her scars being all people could see, that it had taken her a moment to notice that he didn't seem to see the scars. He looked through them to see her.

In fact, her ex-boyfriend hadn't even been able to look at her after the fire and had moved out of their apartment while she was still in the hospital.

She really could have done with his support, and hadn't realised he was so shallow.

Pride kept her from phoning him.

But at that moment, she could see an end to her loneliness.

That the scars might not matter to someone else.

If she gave someone the chance, they might want to get to know her better.

Maybe that someone could be Jude Webb; he might want to date her.

And maybe touch a little more than just her feet and legs.

She'd like that too.

Was she brave enough to ask him out for a drink?

Not just a latte in the cafe on the ground floor of his building, but a proper drink in the fashionable bar further down the laneway.

Maybe some dinner.

She stretched her arms and legs out in front of her, imagining a more intimate end to the evening.

But the scars pulled her up with a sharp pain, reminding her what she'd lost.

Wishful thinking couldn't change the fact of her condition.

She decided to cut and run. It seemed he had everything he needed, she could send him an email to apologise later.

She was halfway back into her jeans, getting ready to take off when he walked through the door holding a jar of cream.

"Sorry to take so long, I had to—," his voice and steps trailing to a standstill.

Rosa clutched at the blanket to hide herself, and tried to say something, "I..."

She realised she didn't have the words to describe what she was feeling, so she turned away.

He dropped the cream, and in three large steps had crossed the workroom, circled her with his arms, and drew her back against his chest, "I understand."

All the pain and frustration she'd felt since the fire consumed her, and she sobbed; harsh guttural convulsions.

Her legs lost all their strength and she would have fallen if he hadn't caught her and gently lowered her to the floor.

As it was, she folded herself around her knees, not really aware he'd tucked between his legs. He cradled her with one arm, and patted her back with the other, one strong pat following a second or two after the one before.

It was calming, and after a time, she stopped crying.

"I'm sorry," she said, not game to raise her head.

He didn't stop patting, "you've been through a lot, I expect it comes out when you least expect it."

She snorted, then sniffed, then reached for her bag for a tissue.

A clean white handkerchief, smelling of laundry soap, sunshine and lavender was pressed into her hand.

"Thank you," she said, and blew her nose three times until it was clear.

Still looking at the floor, and not at him, "does this happen to you all the time?"

"No. My customers are usually businessmen who think they're more special than they are."

She sat up, and he let his arm fall away. She looked into his face, almost level with hers and full of compassion.

"Then how do you come to make shoes for people like me?"

"Heroes you mean?"

She flapped her hand in irritation with him, "anyone would have done the same."

"That's not true, you're one in a million. How many people were waiting at the bus stop with you?"

She scrubbed her face with both hands and then went a little further to scratch her head. Drooping in the face of his admiration.

"Being a hero costs more than you might think."

"I know."

"The medals don't mean shit when you lose your job and people turn away in disgust."

"I know."

"How do you know?"

"My mother was in an industrial accident. She found it hard in the beginning, but her counsellor told her that people were afraid it could happen to them. That she was a visual reminder they should enjoy the good times, and the bad times, and cherish one another."

"I like it," she sighed and looked out the window at the cloudy sky. "Cherish. There's not enough cherishing in the world."

"On that subject," he reached for the cream and waggled it at her, "scar massage?"

"I should go."

"There's no should here. No obligations, no duty, no propriety. There are only choices here. The choice to leave, or the choice to stay."

"But your work!"

He laughed, "I'm charging hideous amounts of money to make shoes by hand, and I have a waiting list of months. I think I can spare a few hours with you."

"It's not going to take hours is it?" she asked, horrified at the thought.

"No. You probably won't be able to take much more than a few minutes. But I'd like to do something...

"Oh, I don't know," he shrugged, "nice for you."

She looked into his face again, searching for any trace of sarcasm or disdain, but it was as open and honest as when she'd first walked in.

She dared, once more, to imagine something more. Let her imagination flit between Friday movie nights curled up on the couch with him, and Sunday brunches at local cafes.

If she didn't open herself up, she would never know.

What was the worst that could happen? A couple of hours of fun, and decades of loneliness after.

She had no qualms running into a burning building, and yet she was hesitating about this?

It might not be forever, but it would be one step closer to a normal life. There had to be a first, why not him?

She shrugged and unfolded her legs, lifting one slightly higher than the other "help me with these?"

He pulled the hem of the jeans down and off her leg, and then the other, folding them up and laying them aside before smoothing the blanket across her legs.

Then he shucked off his boots, sat cross-legged before her, and drew her feet into his lap.

He rubbed his hands together, then picked up her left foot.

His hands were hot.

"The best results," he said, dipping his fingers into the cream, "is with little circles to break up the scar."

He demonstrated, "then rubbing up and down the scar," he demonstrated that too.

"And a little pinch and release along the length."

He didn't say anything else as he gently massaged her feet and legs.

It did hurt, but it was a good kind of hurt. The kind that suggested growth.

She couldn't say anything for certain about her scars, but she felt her heart unfreeze a little.

"How did you come to make shoes?"

He grinned up at her, "my mother."

"Was she a shoemaker?"

"No. After the accident, she couldn't wear shoes. She's the reason I learned to make shoes. You should meet her, you'd like her."

Rosa didn't ask how he knew that but guessed his mother was an advocate, or social worker, or something.

"As I learnt new things, I used her as my test subject."

"She must have a lot of shoes then."

"A few," he grinned, "not all of them successful. But each pair I make for her means I get better at making shoes for people like you."

He paused, and looked at her, his eyes darkening to chocolate again, "would you maybe like to go out for a drink sometime?"

"How about now?"

He smiled, a long slow smile she might have missed if she wasn't looking at him.

《《 • 》》

Not only did she say yes, but she suggested now!

Jude did an imaginary happy dance.

She was easily the most intriguing person he'd ever met.

Stubbornly closed off and independent, with a hint of something softer inside.

Like bitter, dark chocolate with a gooey sweet caramel centre.

"This is just a way to avoid the pain of the massage, right?" he asked.

"Oh no, it's wonderful - you could do my whole body and I wouldn't complain."

He looked up at her face, a little flushed, lips parted, eyes brilliant.

The Rosa who'd walked in the door might have blushed and turned away, but something had happened to that Rosa, and this new Rosa looked at him boldly.

Challenging.

Her challenge pushed all the oxygen out of the room, and he was gasping for air.

Trying to remember why he shouldn't kiss her.

She leaned forward.

Just a fraction, but it was enough.

He reached out to grasp her arms, she fell into his embrace and kissed him.

He stopped thinking.

《《 • 》》

Sometime later, he pushed his hand up her leg, glossed over her bare hip and around her waist in a loose hug.

He kissed her shoulder and nuzzled her neck.

"About that drink?"

She rolled over to face him, cupping his face in her hand as she kissed him.

He tightened his grip, prepared to dally on the workshop floor a bit longer.

"Just a drink?" she said

"Actually, I was thinking about a bite of dinner as well."

"I could eat."

"At a restaurant? Or perhaps somewhere more intimate?"

"Did you have somewhere in mind?"

"There's a small Spanish restaurant in the Lane, we could get some tapas."

"I could eat tapas."

He masked a sigh with another kiss. He'd been afraid she wouldn't want to be seen in public with him.

Or worse, that she'd want to leave.

But he wasn't going to let her walk away without a fight.

"Can I help you dress?"

She froze for a moment, considering her options. Perhaps the bold Rosa had already left.

"Sure," she finally replied.

And a short while later, he realised the problem was the skinny jeans. Almost impossible to get into with any dignity remaining.

"Not much elastic in these suckers," he commented.

She laughed, "no. That day my clothes literally melted on my body, I'm not letting that happen again.

He paused to kiss a scar. "You've been through a lot."

"It could have been worse."

He wrapped her half-naked body in his arms, "you make me want to be a better man."

She accepted his tight hug, "you're already a better man than most.

"Now, about that dinner."

They quickly finished dressing.

As they left, he locked the door, and set the alarm.

"Was the door unlocked the whole time?"

He grinned, "yep."

"Anyone could have walked in anytime?"

"Yep."

"But..."

He paused to let her say more, and when she didn't, he kissed her again. "You're a bit of a daredevil, aren't you?"

"I hadn't for one moment thought you hadn't locked the door."

"To have locked the door when I came back would have been presumptuous."

She gave him a look that would have made lesser men quail, but he just laughed, took her hand and led her down the stairs.

The Spanish restaurant was delightful.

He ordered *mojitos*, olives, spicy chips, grilled eggplant and capsicum infused with garlic and parsley, *jamón iberico* and *chorizo* croquettes, and oysters.

They drank, and ate, and laughed.

She had a dry, acerbic sense of humour, and he wondered if she'd always been that way, or if it was a defence she'd picked up along the way.

And yet there was truth in her observations about life and people.

He covered her hand with his, and she didn't draw it away.

She tucked his hair behind his ear so she could see his face.

He leant across the table and kissed her.

《《 • 》》

Rosa stretched, and this time, her scars didn't pull her back.

She felt pleasantly stretched and exercised. Maybe there was something to the scar massage after all.

Or maybe there was something to him.

After dinner they'd walked to his art deco apartment, stopping for gelato on the way.

And she'd spent the night there.

His apartment was strangely calming. White walls, the bare essentials for furniture, and next to no clutter. Nothing to detract from the large, vibrantly coloured paintings on the wall.

Somehow, it was exactly like him.

And now, somehow, it was exactly like her.

The thought of returning to her cramped and claustrophobic apartment was horrifying.

It had been less than 24 hours since she'd met Jude Webb, but he had rescued her from her bleak existence.

After all that happened the day before, could she let him go?

She'd thought it would be easy, but he was under her skin now.

Rosa turned to speak to him, but the bed was empty.

She sat up and found the room was empty as well.

A door slammed, and she smelled coffee.

"I didn't know if you'd like a latte or an espresso, so I got both."

She grinned as he walked in with a cardboard tray of coffee, and a couple of pastries and sat on the bed.

"Latte," she said, "no sugar."

He twisted the tray so she could pick a coffee up, and after she'd taken her first sip, twisted it back to offer the pastry.

"Actually, I prefer a more savoury breakfast," she said taking a bite, "but somehow this is perfect."

He took a drink of his coffee, "must be the company," he said, toeing off his shoes and reclining on the bed next to her.

"'Spect so," taking another bite.

The last couple of years had been hard, and sitting there, in his bed, she realised that if she didn't take the chance, she would regret it forever.

Nothing ventured, nothing gained - wasn't that what they said?

"Do you have any plans for today?"

"Nothing I can't cancel," he said, "what did you have in mind?"

"Well, I might start with a long, hot shower, and see what happens. Would you care to join me?"

"I'm in," he said, "I'm all in."

THE END

ABOUT THE AUTHOR

Alexandria Blaelock writes stories, some of them for *Ellery Queen's Mystery Magazine* and *Pulphouse Fiction Magazine*. She's also written four self-help books applying business techniques to personal matters like getting dressed, cleaning house, and feeding your friends.

As a recovering Project Manager, she's probably too fond of sticking to plan. She lives in a forest because she enjoys birdsong, the scent of gum leaves and the sun on her face. When not telecommuting to parallel universes from her Melbourne based imagination, she watches K-dramas, talks to animals, and drinks Campari. At the same time.

Discover more at www.alexandriablaelock.com.

BOOKS BY
ALEXANDRIA BLAELOCK

SHORT STORY COLLECTIONS

The Histories of Hayward Hall
Lovelorn, Lovestruck and Love at First Sight
Common or Garden Variety Heroes
Case Files of the Wilkinson Detective Agency
Unavoidable Fates
Christmas Travesties
Five Faces of Felicia Clarke

OTHER FICTION

That Love Nonsense

MS BLAELOCK'S BOOKS

Stress Free Dinner Parties
Signature Wardrobe Planning
Holistic Personal Finance
Minimally Viable Housekeeping
Planning a Life Worth Living

SELECTED SHORT STORIES

Alma's Grace
Balancing the Book
Carmelita Basingstoke
Fate in Your Hands
Kiss of Death
Lady of the Looking Glass
Life in the Security Directorate
Long Weekend in the Snow
Love in the Past Tense
Love in the Security Directorate
Morning Star, Evening Star, Superstar
Needy Bitch
Payton's Run
Phoenix Child
Secret Singer
Shining Star
Ship in a Bottle
Simone Says Hands in the Air
Special Relativity in Space
The Bygone Boyfriend
The Day the Schedule Broke
The Ghost Detectors
The Guardian's Vigil
The Mince Pie Mystery
The Mystery of the Master Suite
The Pseudonym's Bride
The Shadow Thieves
The Time-Space Paradox
Toy Soldiers